CONTENTS

First Published 2002 by Brown Watson
The Old Mill, 76 Fleckney Road,
Kibworth Beauchamp, Leics LE8 0HG

ISBN: 978-0-7097-1474-3

Now I Can
READ
15 Animal Stories

Stories by Maureen Spurgeon
Illustrations by Stephen Holmes

Brown Watson
ENGLAND

HAYSTACK HUNT

'I put it in my pocket!' The farmer sounded cross about something! 'Where CAN it be?'

'It is like looking for a needle in a haystack!' said his wife.

'You are right,' said the farmer. 'A needle in a haystack...'

'A needle!' said Donny Donkey. 'So that is what the farmer has lost!'

'He must have lost it in that big haystack!' said Guppy Goat. 'Let us look!' So they looked all around the big haystack.

Then Donny scrabbled with his hoofs and made the hay fly about. But there was no needle.

Guppy dug into the haystack with his horns. Bits of hay flew about. There was no needle. But there was an untidy heap of hay where the haystack had been!

'We must find the needle soon!' Donny panted. 'Then just think how pleased the farmer will be!'

The farmer did not look pleased!

'What have you done to my haystack?' he roared. 'Look...'

He bent down to pick something up.

'The key to my tractor!' he cried. 'It must have fallen out of my pocket at hay-making!'

Donny and Guppy looked at each other. 'Farmer was cross,' said Donny. 'Then he was pleased.'

'It was not a needle he lost,' said Guppy, 'but a key.'

'And the key was not to open a door,' said Donny, 'but a tractor!'

'It is such a puzzle,' said Guppy at last. 'We need a feed of hay to help us work it out!'

READ THESE WORDS AGAIN!

pocket   sounded
cross   something
donkey   goat
scrabbled   hoofs
horns   untidy
panted   pleased
roared   puzzle

WHAT CAN YOU SEE HERE?

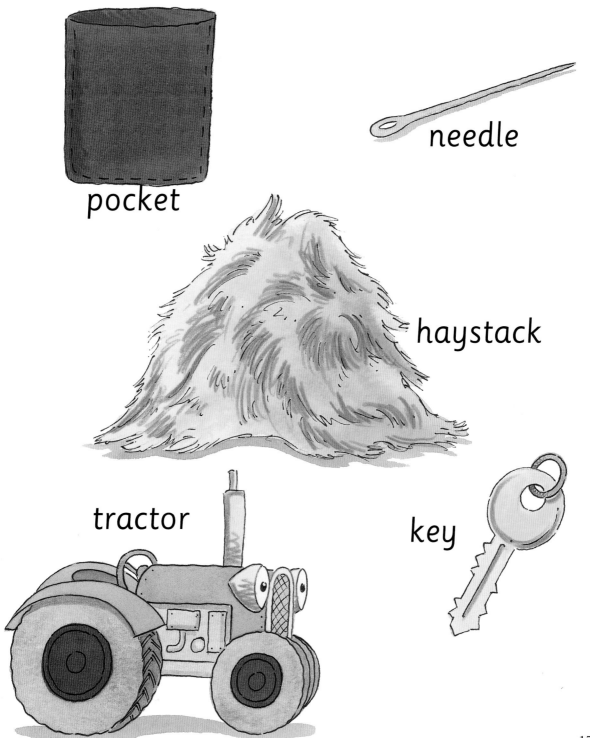

pocket

needle

haystack

tractor

key

13

COPY-CAT CLARA COW

Clara Cow liked to be just the same as Cora Cow. If Cora went into the meadow, so did Clara. If Cora had a nap, Clara had a nap.

'Moo!' went Cora Cow.

'Moo!' went Clara Cow.

'You are a copy-cat, Clara!' mooed Cora. 'You copy everything I do!'

'Clara just wants to be like you, Cora!' said the farmer. 'There is no harm in that!' He held up two cowbells, each tied on a ribbon.

'A bell for you, Cora!' he said. 'And one for you, Clara!'

Clara was very pleased. Cora was very cross!

'You will each have a calf soon!' said the farmer. 'Maybe Clara will have her calf on the same day as you, Cora!'

This made Cora feel even more cross! 'Why must Clara copy me all the time?' she said to herself. 'I hope Clara has her calf first! Then she cannot copy me!'

But Cora was the first cow to have her calf. 'What a fine calf!' said the farmer.

'Moo!' went Cora, very loudly indeed. 'Look again!'

So he looked again. And there, just getting up on its wobbly legs was a second calf, just the same as the first!

'Twin calves!' cried the farmer. 'Well done, Cora!' He was very pleased. But not as pleased as Cora!

'Twin calves!' she mooed. 'Clara Cow cannot copy THAT!'

READ THESE WORDS AGAIN!

meadow	mooed
copy	everything
harm	ribbon
pleased	cross
first	cannot
loudly	indeed
wobbly	second

WHAT CAN YOU SEE HERE?

cowbells

cow

farmer

twin calves

calf

THANK YOU, TRACTOR!

Joey was the pet rabbit at Brad and Mary's school. They were looking after it over the holidays.

'He hates the noise of Dad's new tractor!' said Mary. 'Never mind, Joey! You are safe with us.'

But next day, when Brad and Mary went out into the yard, the hutch was open! Joey had gone!

'A fox has gnawed the latch on the hutch!' said their dad. 'Now we shall have lots of wild rabbits running all over the farm!'

'We will find him!' said Mary. 'Fetch the pet carrier, Brad!'

But there was no sign of Joey.

'That noisy tractor!' said Mary. 'How can Joey hear us calling?'

Suddenly the noise stopped. 'Come on, tractor!' said the farmer. He turned the key to start the engine, but the tractor did not go.

Then, Brad and Mary saw a little, white, fluffy tail. 'Joey!' they cried. 'He is under the tractor!'

'Stay where you are!' called their dad 'Give me the pet carrier!'

'Joey's nose is twitching!' said Brad. 'He is coming out!'

They held their breath. Joey went into the pet carrier and their dad closed the door. 'Keep him in this until I mend the hutch!' he said. 'Now let me see to this tractor!'

He went to the tractor, got into the driver's seat and turned the key. And, the tractor started up as if nothing had happened!

'Look!' said Mary. 'When Joey was under the tractor, it did not budge! Thank you, tractor!'

READ THESE WORDS AGAIN!

school	holidays
gnawed	wild
fetch	noisy
turned	key
engine	under
called	give
twitching	budge

WHAT CAN YOU SEE HERE?

tractor

hutch

rabbit

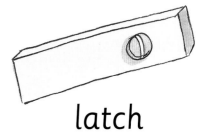

latch

pet carrier

DOWN BY THE LAKE

'Pam!' Sam the shepherd called to the stable-girl. 'A fence has blown down by the lake!'

Letty Lamb heard him. 'Cora Cow!' she cried. 'I have some important news!'

'Important news?' said Cora. 'What is it?'

Letty tried to think. 'Er, there are grown men down by the lake!'

Soon, Cora saw Donny Donkey.

'Donny!' she cried. 'I have some important news!'

'Important news?' said Donny. 'What is it?'

Cora tried to think. 'Er, a brown hen went round by the lake!'

'What news!' said Donny.

'Dinky Dog!' cried Donny. 'I have some important news!'

'Important news?' said Dinky Dog. 'What is it?'

Donny tried to think. 'Er… a man lost a pen by the lake!'

'What?' barked Dinky. She ran all the way to the lake. 'Where is Sly Fox and his den?' she panted.

'Sly Fox and his den?' said Donny. 'You mean, a lost pen!'

'Lost pen?' mooed Cora. 'You mean a brown hen!'

'Brown hen?' bleated Letty Lamb. 'You mean, grown men!'

'Sly fox?' said Sam. 'Lost pen? Brown hen? Grown men? A fence has blown down by the lake!'

The animals looked at each other.

'That is JUST what we were saying!' said Letty.

'Good!' said Sam. 'You can all help us to mend it!'

34

READ THESE WORDS AGAIN!

called	blown
important	news
grown	tried
soon	think
panted	donkey
bleated	looked
were	saying
good	all

WHAT CAN YOU SEE HERE?

fence

brown hen

lake

stable-girl

animals

PIGEONS TO THE RESCUE!

Brad and Mary were at an old windmill with Pam, the stable-girl. Once, the mill had ground corn to make flour. It had been empty for a long time, but Pam's Dad hoped to get it working again.

'Then we can use fresh flour in the bakery next door!' he said. 'Now, I must inspect the roof!'

'Take care, Dad,' said Pam. 'Come on, kids, time to go home!'

As they went outside, there was a loud flutter of wings.

'Sam's racing pigeons!' said Pam. 'They are flying back home!'

They saw Sam the shepherd as Pam drove the jeep into the yard.

'Sam!' said Brad. 'We saw your pigeons near the old windmill!'

'But my pigeons are not back!' said Sam. 'Where have they gone?'

They went to Sam's pigeon loft, at the top of an old barn. They waited and waited. Then, there was a flutter of wings. In flew a pigeon and perched on a ledge. On its leg there was a note.

The note read:

PLEASE HELP. I AM ON A LEDGE IN THE OLD MILL. PAM'S DAD.

Sam called the fire service! Before long, firemen had put up a long ladder to reach Pam's Dad.

'I was near the roof and some of the steps crumbled away!' he said. 'Thank goodness I got Sam's pigeon to carry a message!'

'It did not win a race,' said Brad.

'There will be other races,' said Sam. 'Just as long as they do not stop at the windmill too often!'

READ THESE WORDS AGAIN!

ground	flour
fresh	loud
outside	flutter
wings	racing
loft	waited
perched	ledge
note	firemen

44

WHAT CAN YOU SEE HERE?

old windmill

flour

bakery

pigeons

jeep

SOMETHING LUCKY

One evening, just as supper was ending, Pixie Puppy and Dinky Dog began to bark. 'Woof-Woof!'

'What is it?' said the farmer. 'Someone trying to steal sheep?' He went out and looked around.

'The animals are quiet,' he said at last. 'But, Dinky and Pixie must have heard something!'

Next day, Brad and Mary found a hole in the hedge. 'Someone has been here,' said the farmer. 'It is near the sheep pen, too.'

'No sheep are missing!' said Sam the shepherd. 'I have just checked.'

The next strange thing was a lot of holes in the vegetable patch and a line of carrot-tops out in the lane! Here, they found a little pony, with scratches on its back and sores on its legs.

'Poor little pony!' said the farmer. 'It looks as if someone has just turned him loose. Go and ask Mum to mix some bran mash, Mary.'

'And I will fetch some water for it to drink,' said Brad.

The pony ate a dish of bran mash and drank the water. Then Mary and Brad led it into the meadow.

'I shall ask the vet to give him a check-up,' said the farmer. 'But I think he will be all right. It was lucky for him that he found us!'

'Lucky for us, too!' said Brad.

'That can be his name!' cried Mary. 'Lucky the Pony!'

Lucky stepped close to Mary and nodded his head. Then he nuzzled Brad's hand, just to show that he already felt at home on the farm!

READ THESE WORDS AGAIN!

evening   supper
steal   heard
hole   hedge
checked   found
scratches   sores
loose   bran
mash   lucky

52

WHAT CAN YOU SEE HERE?

vet

sheep pen

vegetable patch

carrot-tops

animals

PIXIE THE PUPPY

Pixie Puppy was a mucky pup! He splashed through mud. He padded through the dirt. He dashed through all the muck and mess.

'That Pixie Puppy!' cried the farmer's wife. 'Just look at his muddy paw-marks all over my yard!'

'Dinky Dog!' she called. 'Can you find Pixie? He needs a bath!'

Pixie squeezed through the hedge! He DID not want a bath! Off he went to hide in the stables.

Hector Horse did not see Pixie.

But he heard Dinky barking.

'Hector! Have you seen Pixie Puppy? He needs a bath!'

But Pixie had already jumped through the window. He did NOT want a bath! Off he went to hide in the cowshed.

Pixie was still panting when he heard Hector call out to the cows. 'Cora! Clara! Have you seen Pixie Puppy? He needs a bath!'

Pixie dashed through the door. He did not WANT a bath! Off he went to hide in the barn.

Just as Pixie crept inside, he heard Cora's voice. 'Donny Donkey! Have you seen Pixie Puppy? He really needs a bath!'

Pixie dashed through the door. He did not want a BATH! He wanted to hide somewhere that nobody would think of looking!

He ran into the house. Outside, voices cried, 'WHERE is Pixie Puppy? He needs a bath!' But Pixie was settling down inside a nice, warm bathroom! 'No,' he said. 'They will NEVER find me here!'

READ THESE WORDS AGAIN!

mucky	splashed
through	padded
dashed	squeezed
crept	heard
wanted	somewhere
nobody	looking
voices	warm

WHAT CAN YOU SEE HERE?

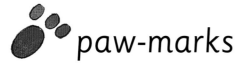 paw-marks

 yard

Pixie Puppy

bath

hedge

THE OLD CARAVAN

There was an old caravan on the farm. It was shabby and broken, but Mary and Brad loved it.

'That old caravan!' said Mum one day. 'It could fall to bits!'

'These winds could blow it over!' said Dad. 'We should break it up!'

'No!' cried Mary and Brad. 'No!'

'All right,' said the farmer. 'I will look at it tomorrow.'

But that night, the winds blew stronger, ripping tiles from the roof and blowing down fences.

It made the caravan rock about so much that its front wheels had broken! What would happen, now?

'Our henhouse was damaged, too!' said Mum. 'All the hens and the chicks have run away!'

Later, Brad and Mary went outside.

'Stay away from the caravan,' said Mum. 'It is too dangerous!'

'All right,' said Brad. 'We will help look for the hens instead.'

They looked in the barn, under the hedges and in the stables. The hens were nowhere to be found.

'Look, Brad!' said Mary. 'Look at our caravan!' They looked. Then they heard clucking! And a fluffy brown head poked out of the window!

'The hens!' cried Brad. 'We must go and tell Dad!' So they did.

'Our hens are safe!' said the farmer. 'The broken wheels made the caravan lower, so they could get inside! Now we could take all the wheels off, to make it safe!'

Brad and Mary cheered! And the hens went on clucking, just to show they loved the caravan, too!

READ THESE WORDS AGAIN!

shabby	broken
could	should
right	tomorrow
night	stronger
ripping	damaged
dangerous	instead
nowhere	fluffy

WHAT CAN YOU SEE HERE?

fence

wheel

old caravan

henhouse

stables

SHEP THE SHEEPDOG

Shep was learning to be a sheepdog. His job was to help Sam the shepherd care for the sheep. But Shep was not good at his job!

'Shep!' cried Sam. 'Do not jump around. That frightens the sheep!'

'Woof!' Shep barked. That made the sheep jump in fright! 'Woof!'

One day, Shep saw a big bird swooping down. 'Woof!' he barked and chased it across the stream. He did not think about the sheep following him!

Then Shep got out and shook himself. Drops of water went all over the sheep. They all ran off.

'Maybe Shep will never make a sheepdog, Sam!' said the farmer.

'But he is a good dog,' said Sam. 'I shall give him one last try.'

Shep heard what Sam said. If only he could show Sam that he could make a good sheepdog!

Just then, his ears pricked up.

'Baa! Baa!' It was a sound Shep knew. 'Baa! Baa!'

Shep squeezed under a hedge.

He ran through a muddy cabbage patch, across the yard and along a path. 'Baa! Baa!' Two sheep had fallen into a ditch!

'Woof!' Shep crouched down beside the ditch, to show that he was taking care of the sheep.

'Shep!' came Sam's voice. 'Your muddy paw prints led me here!'

'Woof!' Shep barked back.

'Silly sheep!' said Sam. He got them out of the ditch. 'Go on, Shep, see them home, boy! I can see you are a sheepdog, now!'

READ THESE WORDS AGAIN!

learning help
fright swooping
barked following
water heard
could squeezed
hedge across
fallen prints

76

WHAT CAN YOU SEE HERE?

sheep

shepherd

big bird

hedge

prints

HECTOR AND THE HORSE SHOW

Hector Horse worked hard on the farm. He pulled the big farm wagons. He cleared away fallen trees. But best of all, Hector liked pulling the plough!

One day, the vet came to see the farm animals. He saw Hector pulling the plough. 'What a fine horse!' he said. 'Why not enter him in the Horse Show?'

'Ooh!' cried Pam the farm girl. 'Can we do that?'

'Yes!' said the farmer. 'But, Pam...'

But Pam was already making plans for the show! 'You must have some ribbons, Hector!' she said. 'I shall plait your tail, and tie bells on your harness!'

Hector gave a loud snort. But Pam put his tail in a plait. She tied bows in his mane and bells on his harness. She was so proud as she led him along, his big hoofs clip-clopping all the way to the show.

'What a fine horse!' everyone said. But Hector did not feel so proud.

'Hello, Hector!' greeted the vet.

'Why are you wearing these fine bows and ribbons and bells?'

'You wanted Hector to enter the Horse Show!' Pam told him. 'This is what show-horses look like!'

'Not for the ploughing contest!' said the vet. He began to take off the bows, the ribbons and bells. 'Come on, Hector! Let us see what a big, strong horse you are!'

After that, Hector won the ploughing contest easily!

'Well done, Hector!' said Pam, proudly. 'What a fine horse you are!'

READ THESE WORDS AGAIN!

worked	pulled
animals	already
bows	ribbons
bells	tail
loud	proud
hoofs	greeted
contest	began

WHAT CAN YOU SEE HERE?

wagon

plough

harness

farm girl

ribbon

85

THE STORY OF THE MILK CHURN

'I shall throw away this old milk churn!' said the farmer's wife. She put it outside the dairy.

The stable-girl was loaded down with hay for Hector Horse. She was glad to see the churn! 'Just the thing to carry the hay!' she said.

She carried it to the stables. Then she emptied it and put it outside.

The farrier had just put some new horseshoes on Hector, when the handle of his tool-bag broke! He was glad to see the milk churn!

'Just the thing to carry my tools!' he said. The farrier rolled the churn full of tools to his car. He put the tools in the boot and left the churn by the gate.

Along came the farmer with a sack of cattle-feed. He was glad to see the milk churn! 'Just the thing to carry this cattle-feed!' he said.

He emptied the cattle-feed into the churn and took it to the cowshed. He emptied the feed into a manger for the cows to eat and left the churn outside.

The churn was under a big tree. It was full of fallen leaves when Brad and Mary found it next day!

'What a nice lot of fallen leaves to take to school!' cried Mary.

They carried the milk churn to the farmhouse. Then they emptied the leaves into a bag and left the churn outside.

'So much junk to get rid of!' said their Mum. She was glad to see the milk churn! 'I am glad I did not throw this old churn away!' she said. 'It is MUCH too useful!'

READ THESE WORDS AGAIN!

thing carry
carried stables
emptied handle
broke tools
boot gate
cattle fallen
leaves useful

WHAT CAN YOU SEE HERE?

farrier

milk churn

horseshoes

tools

manger

SILLY GIDDY GOOSE!

Giddy Goose was so vain!

'See my fine feathers!' she kept saying. 'Look at my lovely long neck! Oh, what a fine goose I am!'

The animals took no notice. They pretended to be busy, saying good night to Cockerel!

'Good night, Cockerel!' said Hetty Hen and Mother Duck.

'Good night, Cockerel!' added Dinky Dog. 'You are a fine bird!'

Giddy did not like this one bit! She was just as fine as Cockerel!

Then she noticed his bright green tail feathers gleaming in the light. Just the feathers for a fine bird!

Giddy waited until Cockerel closed his eyes. Then she crept up and pecked out one, two, three bright green feathers.

'What is that?' cried Cockerel. 'Is Fox about, looking for a fine bird to eat?'

Giddy giggled. Silly Cockerel, thinking she was Fox! She tucked the bright green feathers into her wing.

'How fine I look!' she said.

Fox was on the prowl that night.

He had seen those three bright green feathers!

'Those bright feathers mean a fine supper for me!' he cried, jumping out.

Giddy went stiff with fright! Then, there was a loud hiss and a flash of wings. Mother Goose was hitting out and pecking at Fox!

'Ow! Ow!' howled Fox, and ran off, far away from the farm!

'Silly Giddy!' said Mother Goose. 'You do not need bright tail feathers! But I do not think Fox will be coming back tonight!'

READ THESE WORDS AGAIN!

vain	lovely
notice	pretended
bright	gleaming
pecked	three
giggled	tucked
prowl	night
stiff	fright

WHAT CAN YOU SEE HERE?

night

feathers

Giddy Goose

fox

cockerel

KITTY CAT AND KITTEN

No cat was better than Kitty at catching mice, chasing rats – or teaching Kitten to be a farm cat!

One day, as Kitty was helping Hetty Hen to get the chicks back into the henhouse, she saw a mouse.

'Chase that mouse away from the house!' she hissed at Kitten.

Kitten dashed forward. But Dinky Dog had seen the mouse too. 'Woof-woof!' Her barks scared Kitten.

With a loud 'MIAOW!' she jumped up into a tree.

'Woof!' barked Dinky. 'I did not mean to scare you! Come down, Kitten!' She jumped up at the tree. But Kitten climbed even higher.

'Come down, Kitten!' mewed Kitty. She began to climb the tree. But Kitten climbed even higher.

Brad came along with Hector Horse.

'Kitten!' he cried. 'Jump down on Hector's back!' But Kitten climbed even higher.

'I know!' cried Mary. She went to get some fish and milk. 'Here, Kitten!' she called. 'Come down!'

Kitten stopped. She looked down. Then a bundle of fur and a fluffy tail streaked down the tree and Kitten jumped to the ground!

'Good Kitten!' cried Brad. 'You saw the food Mary got for you!'

But Kitten did not look at the food! She was getting a lost chick into the henhouse, just like Kitty!

'THAT is why Kitten came down!' said Mary. 'Because she saw that chick! Clever Kitten!'

And Kitty stroked her whiskers to show that she quite agreed.

READ THESE WORDS AGAIN!

better	catching
chasing	teaching
hissed	dashed
scared	climbed
even	higher
know	bundle
fluffy	because

108

WHAT CAN YOU SEE HERE?

mouse

Kitty Cat

Kitten

mice

whiskers

A DRAGON ON THE FARM!

One day, Cora Cow was at the stream. Suddenly two big, round eyes stared up at her.

'Moo!' went Cora. 'A dragon!' She ran away in fright!

'Baa!' went Letty Lamb. 'What is wrong, Cora Cow?'

'There – there is a dragon in the stream!' stammered Cora. 'With eyes as big as – as marbles!'

Letty looked into the stream. Two big, round eyes stared up at her! Green claws stretched out!

Letty and Cora ran away in fright!

'Hey!' went Guppy Goat. 'What is wrong, Letty and Cora?'

'There – there is a dragon in the stream!' stammered Cora. 'With eyes as big as – as saucers!'

'And green claws, as long as – as snakes!' cried Letty.

Guppy looked into the stream. Two big, round eyes stared up at him! Green claws stretched out. Long legs waved about! Guppy, Letty and Cora ran away in fright!

'What is wrong?' said Pixie Puppy.

'There is a dragon in the stream!' said Guppy. 'With claws like a – a tiger!'

'Legs like – like a monster!' added Letty.

'And eyes as big as – as wheels!' ended Cora Cow.

Pixie went to see. Two big eyes stared up at her. Claws stretched out. Long green legs waved about.

'A dragon?' she barked. 'Ha-ha! It is only a little FROG!'

'Well!' said Cora. 'NOW we can all have a nice drink of water!'

READ THESE WORDS AGAIN!

stream	eyes
fright	stared
stretched	claws
tiger	monster
wheels	green
about	barked
little	nice

WHAT CAN YOU SEE HERE?

marbles

dragon

saucers

snakes

frog

DONNY GOES TO HOSPITAL

'Woof-woof!' barked Dinky Dog. 'Someone is at the gate!'

'Quiet, Dinky!' said the farmer. 'It is only Nurse from the hospital!'

'We want Donny at the hospital at one o'clock,' Nurse told the farmer. 'We shall look after him!'

Dinky could not believe it!

'Poor Donny Donkey!' she said to Hector Horse. 'Farmer says he is going to hospital, today!'

'What?' Hector could not believe it! 'We must find him!'

'There he is!' barked Dinky. 'In the field, with Brad and Mary!'

'Let us put these reins on you,' Brad was saying. 'Then we will take you to hospital, Donny!'

'Woof!' barked Dinky. 'Then I am going to the hospital, too! Donny is my friend!'

Mary understood. 'All right, Dinky!' she said. 'You can come with us!'

Dinky worried all the way to the hospital. But Donny plodded on, as if he could not wait to be there!

'This way, Donny!' said Nurse.

She led the way into a garden, with balloons hanging around. There was an ice-cream van and a lucky dip stall and people playing games and winning prizes.

'Welcome to our hospital garden party!' said Nurse. 'Now, who will be first to have a donkey ride?'

All afternoon, Donny enjoyed giving rides to the children and being the star of the garden party.

And Dinky Dog? She still could not believe it!

READ THESE WORDS AGAIN!

could believe
reins friend
understood come
worried plodded
playing wait
garden lucky
prizes party

WHAT CAN YOU SEE HERE?

Nurse

hospital

balloons

children

ice-cream van

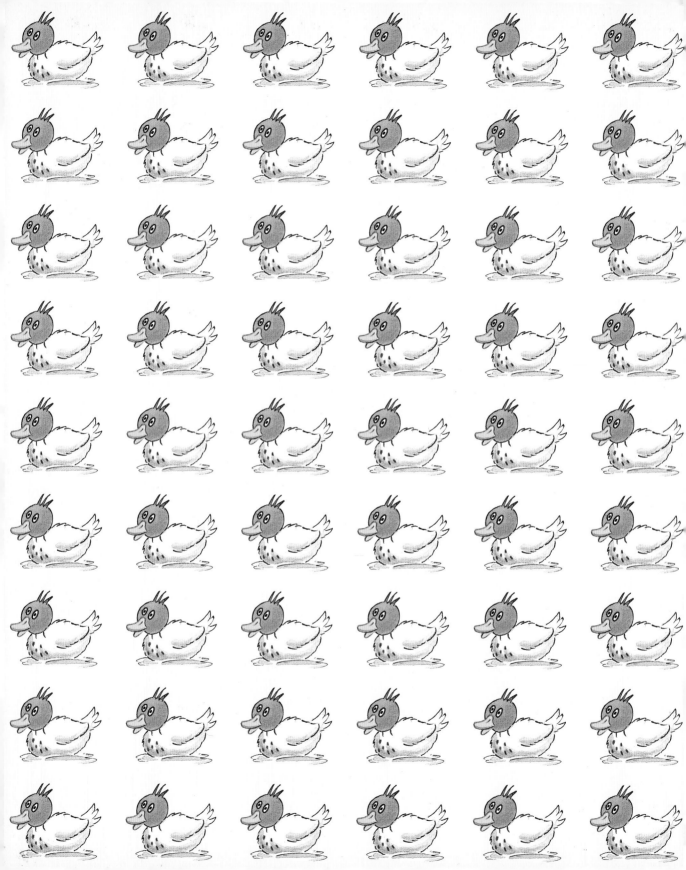